Rat

by Elaine Unger-Pengilly

Illustrated by Marcy Trockstad

Produced by:

FriesenPress

Suite 300 – 852 Fort Street
Victoria, BC, Canada V8W 1H8

www.friesenpress.com

Distributed to the trade by The Ingram Book Company

Table of Contents

1.
In the Beginning

A well-fed rat sat on a hillside. He hid in the growth of brown grasses that moved slowly back and forth in the slight breeze. He licked his coat until it was shining in the autumn sunset. He took a lot of pride in his appearance and always liked to look his best. Today was one of those days. Rat looked great. He felt great. The gray rodent had only one problem. Winter was coming and he needed a nice warm place to live. He needed a place where food would be easy to get and danger would be at a minimum.

He looked down at the farm below. Rat looked over all of the animals in the pasture and in the pens. He saw a small herd of cattle at the far end of the pasture. He watched as a single old horse moved its tail back and forth while standing lazily beside the fence. There were a few chickens in a broken down pen. Then he spotted three goats bucking and pawing and jumping in the last pen.

"GOATS!" thought Rat. "I have never cared

for goats."

He took a few quick steps toward the yard and stopped. He looked and sniffed around for any signs of a big dog or a cat that might be living on the farm. Those animals were dangerous. He couldn't see any. He did see a little mouse as it scampered across the farm yard. The mouse seemed to be heading for the farm house.

"If a mouse can get into that house, then so can I. I'm smart. I'm beautiful. By golly, I'm a beautiful, shiny, smart rat!" he thought. "This farm house would be a great place to spend the cold winter."

Just then, he saw the little mouse change his direction and take cover behind the wheel of a wagon. He must have sensed danger. The door of the house burst open and a woman came outside. She walked quickly toward the garage and opened the large door. She got into a truck and revved the motor. She was out and down the road in no time at all. The farm animals all stopped what they had been doing to watch the vehicle as it went down the road, leaving a thick cloud of dust behind it. The gentle breeze gathered up that dust cloud and slowly mixed it into the air. The haze mingled for a moment before it fell lazily back down to the ground.

The animals went back to their business, except for the goats that must have tired themselves out with their romping games. Two of the three now lay down in their pen. The remaining one was busily chewing on the wooden fence.

"I'd like to chew my way into a home and that silly goat is trying to chew his way out," Rat thought. "I'll never understand goats!"

Just then Rat noticed that the little mouse was scurrying into the garage where the big door had been left open. Rat wondered if there was anything worth investigating in the garage. He waited for a good while to see if something fearful would cause the mouse to race back out. When the mouse didn't come out, Rat became curious.

Again he did a final safety check before he headed down the slope to the garage. Everything was peaceful, so he started his journey down to the farm yard. He moved as quickly as he could. The only thing that slowed him down was his fat belly which rubbed on the ground where any ridges or large rocks jutted up through the soil.

"Perhaps I should have shared that last bag of cornmeal I found. If I hadn't eaten it all myself I wouldn't have such a sack of my own to lug around," he confessed. "Oh well, I look good in my extra fat. That's what's important. Plus I need the bulk for warmth with winter coming on."

2.
Meeting and Eating

When Rat got to the open garage door, he stopped. He sniffed and did a scan of everything around him. Nothing seemed out of the ordinary so he ventured into the garage. He inched his way along the edge in case he needed to dash for cover. He couldn't see the mouse but he could hear him munching on something.

After some further investigating, he found the mouse inside a large thick paper bag that was on the floor near the front of the garage. Rat took a sniff and loved the aroma of the bag's contents. He peered over the top of the bag.

"Hello, little friend," said Rat.

The mouse, so terrified, tried to squeeze his little body inside of itself. Then he hastily tried to crawl up the side of the bag to escape but slipped back down to the bottom again. Next he tried burrowing into the mash that was in the bag. This worked quite well for the little mouse and soon all that was left to see were his little whiskers and nose, panting in and out.

"You can come out of there. I'm not going to hurt you. I'd have to be half starved before I'd eat you!" Rat joked. "Relax! There's more than enough here for the both of us."

The little mouse, coming out of hiding, hoped he would never meet the rat when he was half starved.

"Yikes! I'm a goner if the food runs out!" thought Mouse fearfully.

After a few tries, Rat hopped into the bag and both animals did a whole bunch of munching.

Their ears must have been filled with the sounds of their own chewing because neither rodent heard the truck return until it was moving slowly into the garage. Both huddled and made not a sound. All chewing and pawing had come to a halt. Even their breathing was shallow and soft. The truck door opened and the woman hastily grabbed some bags and something that was whimpering in a cage. She closed the garage door and headed for the house.

"What do we do now?" whispered the mouse.

"You do whatever it is you do," said Rat, thinking only of himself. "I just know what I'm going to do. I'm going to continue to eat until I've had all I can hold. I'll worry about the next part when the next part comes."

This sounded like a reasonable plan to the mouse so

they carried on with their meal.

Finally, after dropping a few pellets of their own, they tried to climb out of the bag. It wasn't possible. They were both too full. They could not hoist the weight of their own bodies out of the bag without the sides of the bag giving way on top of them. Out of pure exhaustion from all the effort they both lay down for a rest.

3.
Mouse's Exit or Escape

Night came and passed. The dim morning light was coming in through the garage windows before either animal awoke. Rat woke first. After a few stretches he got up and had another nibble or two before thinking about his next move.

Finally, he said, "Wake up, little friend. It will take the both of us working together to get out of here. We are going to have to run at the side of the bag with all our weight until it tips over. Do you understand the plan?"

Mouse understood nothing. He still had half a dream to finish. Rat gobbled away at the mash until the mouse had roused himself for the morning ahead.

"I'm thirsty," said the mouse with a croaky morning voice.

"All the more reason to get out of this bag," declared Rat.

Now that the mouse was fully awake, Rat explained the plan again. His plan did not work. There was no room to run inside the bag so they jumped and they vaulted and kept on until finally the side of the bag began to tear away where their little claws had pierced it time and time again.

The new plan was as good as the first! Soon the bag ripped open enough for them to simply hop out. The mash spilled out behind them.

"That's great! The next time we decide to meet for a late lunch at this particular diner the food will be waiting for us on the floor," said Rat. "How perfect is that?"

The mouse made no comment. He was intent on finding water and he thought he'd have to get out of the garage to do it.

Rat was in no hurry to leave. He had a full belly and was quite happy to explore the rest of the garage before moving on. After all, this might be his future winter home. If it was going to be this easy to get a good meal and shelter from the cold what more could he want? Perhaps a nice warm, cozy bed, and for all he knew the bed could be here just waiting for him.

While the mouse leapt and slammed his body up against the garage door in an attempt to escape, the rat took a tour of the garage.

"What is he thinking?" thought Rat. "He probably weighs less than a half an apple. He'll bust his bones before he busts down that garage door. Too bad he's only as smart as half an apple!" He snickered at his cruel humor.

Among some old jars and lids Rat found enough liquid for his morning drink. From behind him came the rasps of a very thirsty mouse.

"There's no way out!" gasped the mouse. "I have to find water!"

"No fear," said Rat. "There's water enough right here in this lid. I've had my fill, so help yourself."

The little mouse drank and drank until finally he raised his head.

"Was that water?" he asked. "…tasted more like rotten lemons…

with molasses." Mouse puckered up his little face.

"It was wet, wasn't it?" sassed Rat. "You certainly are fussy for being such a little fur ball! Do you often mix your rotten lemons with molasses? How would you know what that would taste like?"

Mouse made no comment. He just shrugged his shoulders.

Rat continued to explore the contents of the garage. He climbed into low boxes and came back out. He disappeared behind pieces of machinery parts and came out the other side. The little mouse sat quietly cleaning his whiskers and watched as Rat went from one corner of the garage to the next, and the next, and finally to the last.

"I might be home. This might be the winter apartment I've been saving up for," Rat announced. "This is definitely enough for me, though I don't think it would be suitable for the both of us, so run along now. Perhaps some time in the way-out-there future you can pop by for lunch. Or NOT! If you're too busy or too far away I'll certainly understand. So it was nice dining with you. Now off you go! May we never meet again."

The little mouse made no comment. After making a more slow and careful examination of the garage door he found a corner where the weather stripping was chipped. He was able to slither under the crack to get out. Away he went without a farewell.

"Good riddance!" thought Mouse. "He was scary!"

Rat hardly noticed the mouse had gone. He was far too busy imagining how he could organize everything for his new winter home. He had left several piles of his own pellets to claim his territory and was feeling quite smug and content.

"Snow? Cold? Blizzards? Bring it on, Old Man Winter!" he said with excitement. "I'm ready!"

4.
Hello Pup

Autumn was turning into winter. Several times there had been some mild skiffs of snow on the window ledges. The snow melted off during the day's sunshine but the nights were getting chillier.

Life wasn't perfect in Rat's garage-apartment but it was pretty good. He had enough mash to give him meals for quite a while. He had chewed apart an old sack and some other choice materials to build a warm nest behind a large box that was filled with old lumber.

One day the woman left her truck door open. When she had gone into the house with her hands full, Rat explored the inside of her truck. He found that the material on the underside of the truck seats provided a wonderful final touch to his nest. He pawed away at the soft lining until he had quite a pile of it. Then, slow trip after trip, he moved it to his nest.

During one of his adventures around the garage he discovered several different liquids to drink. Some were thick and made him feel ill. Others were bearable and there was one that made him quite giddy. He could have his choice, depending on the mood he was in.

It was a good life until the day the woman decided to clean the garage. She brought along the whimpering thing in the cage. How annoying was that? The woman backed her truck out and began sweeping the garage floor. Suddenly she shrieked and started carrying on about the little pellets that Rat left when and wherever he felt the need. She started to do a more thorough search of the place. She found the ripped bag of mash and other bits of evidence of Rat's existence, like tiny pieces from the underlining of her truck seats.

"Rats!" the woman screamed. "I won't have rats living in here!"

She hurried to her truck and zoomed away. In her haste, she forgot about the cage which she usually carried around with her like it contained a baby. Rat used this time to explore the cage and its contents. By golly, it was a baby! A baby dog to be exact!

"Oh, no!" thought Rat. "This woman is concerned she might have a rat in her garage but look at the far more wretched thing she has in the cage! Doesn't she realize what it will become?"

Rat leaped at the cage that held the sleeping pup until he awoke. The pup cocked its head from side to side trying to place Rat in his animal memory bank. When he wasn't able to, he began to wail like a baby.

Rat stopped throwing his body against the cage. The pup continued his short little gasps and screams as Rat sat quietly and made weird faces at him.

What was Rat to do? How could he end this non-stop whining? The sound was starting to get on his nerves! Rat tried a few of his sweeter poses. Then he tried his tough-love look. When none of his best attempts worked he hung on the side of the cage and rattled it. He teased the pup with every kind of sound he could come up with. This only made matters worse.

Rat was a tad hungry from putting on such a great act. He went to fill up on the mash in the bag. After a while the pup fell into another nap and continued to sleep his life away until the woman returned. Rat quickly dashed to the safety of his nest.

The woman was on a mission to end Rat's life. She put down special pellets and traps. Then she removed the half-eaten bag of mash. She stormed around, banging and cleaning until her job was complete. Then she grabbed up the cage with her miniature mutt, stomped out and slammed the garage door.

Rat came out of hiding. He knew all about poison pellets. Some of his relatives had been tricked by the aroma so he knew better than to take the bait. He would also have to move very carefully now that there were traps around.

He examined every new thing with his keen nose

and eyes. His little apartment wasn't feeling nearly as close to perfect as it had earlier that morning. Rat went to bed with an empty stomach that night, which was rare for him. He would have to remind himself not to eat the poisonous pellets when he woke up hungry.

Rat's life had changed that day and it hadn't been a change for the better. The woman would return to do war with him until one of them finally won. Rat never thought of himself as a loser. He needed a new plan.

5.
Grumbling Goats

Rat was quite clever and he often reminded himself of just that. He had already set off two of the traps that had been meant to end his life. He had done this by finding pieces of leftover wood chips and dropping them onto the traps from up above.

The woman had cleaned the garage of all other wood pieces and leftovers. She had swept all extras away with her long handled weapon. The materials for setting off any more traps were impossible to find now.

That was only one of Rat's problems. The far greater problem was his lack of food. Without the bag of mash he was running low on energy and he could only live off his own fat for so long. The winter winds were setting in and the extreme chill seemed to be getting inside his bones.

Often the garage door was left open. If the coast was clear Rat scurried out to the goat's pen where he rummaged through their food to find any small morsels that were pleasing to him. He had tried to take over the chicken pen too but the old white hens made such a fuss with all their cackling he was afraid it would alert the woman.

Oats and hay would have to do for now. One of the goat kids tried to butt him and make a game out of his long tail. He had to put on his seriously mean face and hiss like a snake to get out of the pen alive. The old mother goat had the nerve to threaten him once he was safely on the outside of their pen.

"If you come back here we'll pick you up by your long leathery tail and flip you until we hear your neck crack like a dead twig!" she shrieked. "It will be a game for the kids and I certainly won't stop them. Now get on your way and don't be coming back!"

"I'd like to flip you into next week!" Rat replied as he bravely backed away. "You're already cracked – in the head!" he mumbled but not loud enough for the goat to hear.

6.
Hooting Hens

The garage door had been left open the next day. Rat was so hungry he decided he would have to give the chicken pen another try. The pen was so broken down it was easy for Rat to get in. Once he was in the cackling began. At first it was just the mild cackles of the concerned hens guarding their nests of eggs. Rat climbed up the ramp to the cubicles and crept around from nest to nest.

The memories of the taste of a nice fresh farm egg had him in a trance. He laid down in one of the cubicles which held a nest. He was lying with an egg on either side. Rat was contemplating which one to crack first when a silly old blind hen came and sat down on her eggs and right on him! He rather enjoyed her warmth but he was getting that uncomfortable closed-in feeling he so disliked. He was in darkness under the hen and he couldn't get any air! He started to panic! This was not good.

He had to take action and take it fast. He used all his

strength to lift his body in a quick upward bolt. This caused the old hen to rise up and tip as if on a pedestal. Then she lost her balance and shot out the front of the cubicle and into the air!

Now chickens are not known for their ability to fly but this old bird seemed to be doing a pretty good job of flapping her wings while somersaulting toward the ground. She was croaking and cackling all the way down when she landed on the top of another hen. This caused the old blind one to flap her wings and take to the air once more. Now she was somersaulting off the top of every third or fourth bird until she finally hit the floor with a THUD! This was enough to get all the hens in an uproar of cackles and hoots.

Rat couldn't stand all the noise! He wasn't his brave and confident self as he shuddered and shimmied his way out of the pen amidst the uproar of noise. This had not been the pleasant experience he had planned. As he scurried away he could hear the mother goat hollering after him:

"What I told you earlier goes for the hens as well. We will finish you off and it won't be pretty. LEAVE US ALONE!"

"I could finish you off in my sleep!" he sassed back. He didn't mean it though. He couldn't rule over goats and he knew it.

Once he was back in the safety of his own nest

behind the lumber box in the garage he could hear the woman racing to the chicken pen and ranting about the noise.

"I should have just chopped off all of your heads in the fall. Then I'd be done with you chickens," she grumbled. "You wouldn't be making this racket if you were in my deep freeze!"

She fed the chickens and they quieted down. The woman closed the garage door on her way back to the house. Rat lay in his nest shivering from the cold and all of the excitement. Perhaps it was also the result of his empty tummy.

"I guess I won't be having eggs for supper," sobbed poor Rat. "I won't be having anything for supper - again!"

He went to sleep hungry and dreamed of eggs: scrambled eggs, eggs easy-over, eggs sunny-side-up, eggs Florentine and even eggs Benedict. Those mouth-watering visions got mixed in with the old hen flapping and tumbling through the air toward Rat. Then it was Rat who was tumbling through the air, easy-over, scrambled, sunny-side-up, hard boiled! Then came the voices: "We'll finish you off! I should have chopped your head off!" Then the lid of a deep freeze closed with him inside.

The dream repeated over and over until finally he awoke with a thud. He scanned the darkness of the garage for a long time before he was able to get back to sleep. He had a very restless night, to say the least.

7. Getting Into the Inn

The only good plan Rat could think of was to get into the house. He could just imagine the warmth and the food. He had to find a way. That same day he had his chance to explore the situation. The woman and her pup had left the farm yard in her truck. The garage door was left open. The whole place was peaceful.

Without his summer camouflage, sneaking up to the house was not as easy. The white blanket of snow on the ground made him stand out like a rat in a pen of white hens. The mere thought of the hens didn't bring him any pleasant memories! He scurried on his way. He was relieved when he got to the edge of the house. He moved slowly around all the sides looking for a way in.

He discovered a trap door that led to the basement. He was examining a puncture in the wooden cover when the old wood cracked. He suddenly lost balance and fell through it! To his surprise, there was no base below him and he ended up bouncing and tumbling down several concrete steps. That hurt! He felt rather injured in both body and pride as he looked around in the dark.

This was not good. There was another door at the base of the steps and it was definitely solid. He was trapped between the two doors and didn't have a hope in getting back out.

"Think, Rat, think!" he said. "I am supposed to be a clever rat but I haven't the foggiest idea how to get out of this. I might still be here in the spring all shrivelled up – starved, frozen and quite DEAD!" He sniffled.

The thought of this horrified poor Rat. His heart raced wildly. He was heading for a panic attack! He took a few slow deep breaths. The odor in the space between the doors was not pleasant. As his eyes became more accustomed to the dark, he was able to see more of his surroundings.

The wretched smell came from a litter box near the edge of one wall. "Does someone live here? Is there another animal in here that I'm not seeing?" he softly asked himself.

He became very still and made a detailed check of the concrete walls, the corners and everything around him.

Finally, he gave a huge sigh. "No, I am quite alone in here. There's really nowhere anyone or anything could be lurking. If I have to take cover there will only be one or two places to hide. The thought of diving into that litter box is clearly too awful but I could possibly fit behind it. If I was thinner this wouldn't be a problem and the longer I stay in here the thinner I'll get! Good grief! What will become of me?" he sobbed.

Just then Rat heard sounds from inside the house. A door slammed. He heard footsteps up above. The human had returned. He heard her voice but it was only a muffle. Before long he heard a scratching on the other side of the door to his death cell and the next thing he knew it opened!

He barely had enough time to take cover behind the litter box. The rays of light from the house blinded him for a second but he was sure he had seen that little mutt. Yes, the mutt was piddling in the litter box!

"How gruesome", thought Rat. "What filthy animals they are, going in the same spot!'

But this was no time to linger on the smell of dog's urine. There might be an opportunity here for him. The door to the house had been left ajar. There was plenty of space for Rat to get through but he had to be quick! He had no time to do any safety checks of what might lie ahead. It was now or never. It was do or die!

Rat decided to DO. He raced from behind the litter box to the sounds of the startled mutt. He shimmied through the partially opened door. He saw a spot of safety under an old couch and he dove for it!

The mutt wailed and barked in an unbearably babyish way right beside Rat's hiding spot. The pup pawed at the side of the couch. One time his paw came close enough to nearly swipe at Rat's nose! Rat moved himself to the center of the space where he felt more protection. Now he could hear the woman coming down the staircase with that cooing tone.

"Oh, what has you so riled, my little angel? Here now, come to Mommy," she said as she bent down to pick up the little beast.

"Blah, blah, blah," thought Rat. "I'm starting to think dogs deserve humans and the other way around too!"

The woman closed the door to the litter box, and puppy in arm, made her way up the staircase to the upstairs and turned out the light. The door closed and Rat could breathe again.

"I'm in!" he said. "My plan was to over-winter in this house and here I am. I should be overjoyed. So why is my heart still racing? Perhaps I've had too much excitement for one day. Eating might calm me down. That's just the way a rat is. So now what?"

8.
A Trap or Two

Rat knew that pups piddled their lives away for their first year so there was no safety near the door that led to the litter box. And whoever heard of a dog using a litter box? Was this woman such a coddler the dog couldn't learn to go outside like most dogs?

"Oh well! Too bad for the pup. At least I get to do my business wherever I want to," admitted Rat.

And speaking of litter, Rat left a bit of his own under the couch before peeking out.

"That must have been one of those nervous pees," he said to himself.

Rat peered out from under the couch. He was in a storage room. He saw pieces of old furniture here and there and towers of boxes upon boxes, the contents of which he was too excited to imagine.

"There will be a whole lot of exploring to do down here," he thought, gazing around the room.

To his dismay there was no smell of food, no aroma of mild decomposition, no hint of anything that might fill the gap in his gurgling belly. There were several other doorways though. Some of them had doors while two just had openings where doors could hang.

"Exploring can be a life's pastime down here," he thought, and the idea excited him "…but food comes first!"

Rat stayed near the walls as he scampered to the first open doorway. Inside the room there was a strong smell of oil used in vehicles. There was a workbench and a lot of tools hanging in spots just made for them. Nothing here caught his interest at the moment, though he thought he might return for a more thorough investigation at a later time.

The other room without a door had the rank smell of clean laundry humans seemed to like so much. Rat had other ideas as to what this room should smell like and he would soon be adding his own scents and aromas to the space.

He carried on to a closed door that had a large gap at the bottom and squeezed underneath it without a problem. Now this was an interesting room. Along one wall was a table from which hung many chewable cords and cables connected to a TV screen. He knew all about TVs from the last home he had been in.

"It's strange how humans are so fascinated with

TV," he noted. "I have never seen anything that's kept my interest. I guess we rats are far more intelligent than people."

He decided this was another room that would require a revisit sometime later. He slapped his tail down in acknowledgement of his great wisdom. He had no idea it had landed in a mouse trap. A loud SNAP was all he heard!

It hadn't hurt him much but when he turned to examine the situation he was not pleased. The mouse-trap was attached to the very end of his tail! He tried to lift his tail but the extra weight made it quite impossible.

"Now this is just great!" he grumbled, dragging the thing across the floor with him. "Wherever I go there will be this annoying clickety-clacking behind me. I won't be able to sneak up on anything, that's for certain. I'll be heard coming from here to the chicken pen!"

The trap was definitely an inconvenience to drag behind him but he knew he wouldn't be able to think of a way out of this until he found something to eat.

He clicked and clacked and shuffled his way under the door and down the hall. When he got to the closed door at the end of a hallway he thought he smelled apples. Now this was a pleasant memory - sweet and very crunchable.

The gap under this door was not as large as the last one. Rat had to empty all the air out of his lungs and make his body no wider than the width of his skull. He jimmied and jammied his way through the narrow gap until he got to the trap on the end of his tail. The trap was too large to move through the opening under the door.

"Oh great!" he blurted. "Now I'm mostly in and part way out!"

He was in a fix. He began to heave and ho with all his might. The smell of food gave him more power than he knew he had. Tug and pull, heave and ho, tug and pull, heave and ho: until finally he heard a snap! The trap gave way and his tail was free! Sprawled out on the floor from exhaustion, he noticed he'd lost several tufts of fur which were now attached to the underside of the door. This saddened him for a moment. It was not pleasant news for a rat who thought so highly of his appearance.

He got back up on all fours to straighten himself out. He did a quick preening job to be sure he was looking his best, though he had to work extra hard at covering the bald spot where his leathery skin now showed. Sadly, he could see his missing fur stuck to the bottom of the door. He examined his long tail to look for any permanent damage caused by the mousetrap. Thankfully, there was none.

9.
Utopia!

He was in and he was looking at the mother lode! There were shelves of jars, all neatly labeled. There were rows of cans. Neither of these excited him that much. Despite his far exceeding intelligence he had never found a way to get into cans or jars.

When he saw the number of boxed and bagged foods, though, he nearly jumped for joy! Some of the food items on the floor had been left in open sacks! He let his nose guide him and dove into the nearest bag where he devoured an apple in seven seconds: munch, munch, munch, gulp!

Rat was reveling in his excitement and accomplishment when he heard a common scratching, and then an ever so familiar munching. He looked high and low but there was no one or no thing to be seen. After a length of silence, the crunching sounds began again.

Following the sounds with his keen ears, he was led to an open sack with a netted texture. Through the holes in the mesh he could see a fast moving jaw and then a tail that had flipped through a hole in the mesh. Rat gave it a friendly nip and the little mouse nearly hit the roof!

"Hello Mouse! How is life in there? And how is life in here?" asked Rat, as he scanned the room with his paw outstretched to indicate that he was referring to the entire place. The little mouse made no attempt to comment until he had chewed and downed the last morsel in his mouth.

"It's good," the little mouse said and continued munching away.

"It's good? That's all you've got? You're in rodent heaven and you can't sing your praises or even stop to show your gratitude? It's only GOOD?" spouted Rat. "I recall you as being one who didn't have much to say. Whole thoughts like 'I'm thirsty' or 'I need to get out of here' or something about rotten lemons: Those were the best I heard from you but this is Utopia! Couldn't you show a bit more enthusiasm?"

"I'm busy," replied the little mouse.

"Well, there we have it! Another two-word answer!" exclaimed Rat. "Eat away then. I'm half starved myself so move over. I'll talk to you later."

The little mouse moved over as far as he could. He didn't like the sounds of the rat being half starved. He had heard that threat before when they had met in the garage! "Yikes! I'm a goner if the food runs out!" the little mouse thought.

Both animals ate until they could eat no more. Without words or common courtesies they belched and went to sleep right where they were.

In spite of nocturnal instincts they slept right through the night and when they arose there was a hint of day-light showing beneath the door. The fur tufts Rat had parted with the day before created interesting little shadows against the dim light under the door.

After much yawning and stretching, Rat got up and started looking around for a more permanent sleeping spot. Not using his brain, he had dangerously sacked out inside a sack. He knew better than to think he would ever let that happen again. If this was Utopia, he wanted to stay alive to enjoy every minute of it.

10.
Hole in the Wall

For the rest of the day Rat sniffed every inch of the food storage room. This was paradise! He also spent time relaxing and recovering from the fears and events of the previous days. He went into great detail to explain his adventure to the mouse, even adding some things that hadn't really happened, just to make his journey seem more exciting. It's not that he was a born liar, though he had told a few in his day. He only did that so it might be a more enjoyable story for Mouse. When his story was done he asked the mouse how he had come to live in the house.

Now Mouse was the sullen type. He minded his own business. He had a bad experience in the past. He had lost his family due to his long and untruthful stories. He had learned his lesson the hard way. Since then he spoke only when necessary and as little as possible.

" ...through the door," replied the mouse. That was all he said.

"Ah, there we have it! Through the door, you say.

You have no clue how to tell a story! Entertain me! Give me more details and something to imagine!"

"Don't want to," the little mouse said. Then he scurried behind a heavy jug with a low spout that leaked ever so slowly, the one that gave him his daily drink of water.

Rat tried to follow him but the mouse had simply disappeared. He was nowhere to be found. Then Rat spied a small hole that had been chewed in the wall just above the baseboard. He put his eyeball up against the hole and discovered the room with all the cords and the TV screen. He was looking in from the underside of the table. Rat had to confess that this was very clever on the mouse's part. This not only gave them a fast get-away but also doubled their living space.

Rat now considered the food storage room to be their kitchen/dining area and this one with the TV screen to be their living room. Rat would never have to lose any more of his beautiful coat trying to slither under the low door to the food storage room. This second room, he recalled, had a door that had much more space underneath.

"Mousy, you're so clever," said Rat with his nose in the hole. "Whatever made you think of this?"

"Didn't. It was already here," said the mouse.

"I should have known there would be a very short explanation," thought Rat. "Well, I'll be joining you in the living room shortly, my little friend."

Unfortunately, Rat could only get his head through the hole so far. The widest part of his skull was right behind his eyeballs and there was no possible way his whole head would fit.

"I can't fit through this hole," said Rat. "Come and help me chew it bigger. You mice are such fantastic chewers."

"Made for a mouse," said his new partner.

"Well, I can see that!" said Rat. "So let's make it bigger so it's made for a rat or a very *fat* mouse!"

"Nope," said the mouse.

"Well, you ungrateful little thing! Look what I did for you in the garage. We were working on a true and deep friendship inside that bag of mash. Have you forgotten all of that?"

"Nope," the mouse said. As he thought back to their time together in the garage he recalled very little that represented friendship.

"Oh, never mind," huffed Rat. "I'll do it myself!"

He chewed for the better part of the afternoon and into the evening before he was happy with the size of the new and improved doorway. By then it was time to eat, so he dove into a bag for a supper of dried corn. The mouse wandered in silently and joined him for his meal.

11.
Outsmarting the Human

The woman had been up and down the stairs several times each day to let the pup into the landing with the litter box. She had not bothered the two rodents and they had not bothered her.

The following day assured them they had nothing to fear. They could hear her come down the stairs. They could hear her in the hallway that led to the food storage room. They could hear her at the storage room door, so they had lots of time to skedaddle through the hole-in-the-wall.

That was when the woman noticed the mousetrap lying on its side. The little pup was about to pick it up in his mouth but the woman stopped him just in time.

"Oh, you could have hurt your mouth. Or you could be wearing that on your little nose! Oh dear me! Give that to me," she said, reaching down for the mousetrap. "You must have dragged this in from the computer room. Well, you're lucky you didn't get it snapped onto your tongue! I guess I can't have anything dangerous lying around now that I have you."

She placed the mousetrap high up on a window ledge. The two rodents heard her go into the food storage room where she gathered up a few cans and jars. Then she closed the door and was gone down the hall and up the staircase with her little mutt by her side.

"This is so perfect," said Rat. "If she comes into our kitchen we'll be in our living room. If she happens to come into our living room we'll move to our kitchen. Oh, what a lovely game! We may never have to see each other at all!"

Winter had set in hard by this time. Some of the old basement windows had thick layers of frost on them and they shook and rattled from the blizzard-like winds. Though there were slight skiffs of snow in the landing where the dog's litter box was, the house was toasty warm and well-insulated from the cold outdoors.

12.
Oh, For a Bit of Jam

Oh, what a glorious life for a little mouse and a beautiful shiny rat! Neither animal felt the need to prepare a winter nest as there were many safe and secluded sleeping spots here and there. They could sleep in a different spot every day of the week before having to revisit one, if they had cared to.

Rat rather liked the warmth of mouse's body when he snuggled up beside him for a nap. Mouse did not and would usually move to a different spot as soon as Rat was asleep. One day, as they were sharing a beautiful lunch of dry oatmeal, Rat asked him about this peculiar habit.

"Mouse, why don't you want to spend your napping time beside me? When I wake you've usually moved to some other spot. What's with that? Why don't you want to stay warm?"

"Don't care to," replied the mouse. Deep inside he thought back to Rat's threat about being half starved. He had visions of himself being eaten up in his sleep! Yikes!

"Could you give me a reason?" Rat asked. He wanted to coax a few more words out of the little mouse.

"Nope," replied the mouse, cleaning his mouth with his little paw. Then he scampered behind the water jug and through their round doorway.

"Sometimes I get the feeling my best friend doesn't really care for me," said Rat to himself. "I'll have to do something wonderful for him so he can admire me the way he should. I guess it's not enough that I found this lovely living arrangement for the two of us. I increased the size of the doorway so it would be easier for him to get through. I usually take all the risks by going first when we go to explore the boxes and chew on the old furniture. Hmm. That's something I'll have to think about: Does he even follow me to the boxes or is he just glad to be rid of me? Does he go somewhere else?"

Rat thought about all these things as he hurried off to see where the little mouse had gone to. He followed him into the laundry room where they had been several times. There was no door to this room. The smell of fabric softener and heavy detergent was slowly being replaced by more pungent odors the two rodents left behind. Rat watched from below as the mouse made his way up a rough table leg, onto the table, then onto a smooth white machine with an open lid.

"Jam! I smell it!" exclaimed the mouse.

"Well, well," said Rat. "That's the most excitement I've ever heard from you."

The woman had preloaded the washing machine with the kitchen dish cloths and towels. From where Rat sat he could smell the slight aroma of the jam dessert. He watched as the mouse took a little leap and disappeared into the drum of the machine. He was debating whether or not to follow when he heard the woman coming down the stairs and toward them. Rat barely had time to take cover behind the detergent boxes on the floor. He was not pleased to have to spend time amidst these harsh smelling odors.

He had never been so close to the woman! She went to the smooth white washing machine and added a few more items she'd brought down with her, then bent down to the detergent boxes. Rat could feel the warmth of her breath! She stood back up. She poured some detergent into the drum of the washing machine, closed the lid, turned a few dials and left the room. Luckily, the little piddler had not come down with her or he would have given away Rat's hiding place for certain. He gave a heavy sigh of relief as he heard her go up the stairs.

Rat listened to the sound of the water filling the wash machine and then went out the open doorway to explore the tool room. It hadn't shown much in the way of interesting items but Rat wanted to make sure. He didn't want to leave any shelf unexplored or any stone unturned as the saying goes. He never gave another thought to what might happen to the mouse. Rat only thought about Rat and that was that.

13.
What a Ride!

The shock-stricken mouse, on the other hand, didn't know what hit him. Only moments ago he had been gnawing on a dish cloth which had small remains of strawberry jam and now he was crouched in total darkness trying to keep his head above water!

As the machine filled with water, the little mouse leapt from one item to another using them as small rafts. This wasn't easy in total darkness. Soon every item was as drenched as he was and there was no way of escaping. Then, after the sound of a single click, came the roaring of the motor. The water began swirling and jugging and the mouse did everything he could to stay afloat.

He swam from rag to cloth hoping one of them would keep him above water. He managed to get some support but basically he was swimming for his life! This motion went on and on for a very long time until the motor finally stopped. Another click was heard and the water began to drain.

"Thank goodness!" gurgled the mouse. "I don't know how much longer I could have faced those rapids!"

Once all the water had drained out, the whole process repeated itself. Water spewed in again. This time the articles were useless as rafts because they were drenched and heavy and stayed near the bottom of the washing machine.

The mouse was doing all he could to keep his nose above water when the motor again clicked in. Back and forth, back and forth, round and round, round and round - the little mouse was about to drown out of pure exhaustion when the motor finally stopped and the water began to drain again. The little guy could not have swum for another minute. After the water had drained, he heard yet another click.

"Oh no!" he sobbed. "Not again!"

But this time the action was different. The motor began to spin and spin more rapidly as small bursts of water spewed into the machine and then drained out. The mouse braced himself against the side, butting up against the laundry to enjoy the ride, if that was even possible. No! There was no enjoyment in this at all!

The mouse could not recall how many more cycles of torture he endured before a very loud click was heard and all went still. Everything inside him had been shaken up and he was extremely dizzy, wet, and beyond tired from his swimming marathon.

As the woman opened the machine lid, he used his last bit of energy to burrow himself between two wet rags. She grabbed the laundry by the handful and with it came the drenched and exhausted mouse. She flung the handful into another machine which had its opening on the front rather than the top.

Just then, there was a ringing sound from upstairs and the woman hurried out of the room and up the stairs with the pup at her heels.

The little mouse sensed a far worse fate was ahead of him if he didn't muster up enough energy to escape through the open dryer door. He struggled up to the opening and gave a final big boost which sent him falling to the floor.

He was injured. He was brutalized. He was drenched and spun dry. He'd had a near-death experience that was for certain! Even so, he was able to push himself slowly across the floor like a wet mop until he lay wasted behind the boxes of detergent. There he stayed and panted, barely alert to what was going on around him.

The woman had hurried back in and had finished loading the wet laundry into the dryer. She turned it on and hurried back out and up the stairs. None of this, including the loud rumbling of the motor, even registered on the little mouse. He slunk and shivered in his hiding place until he fell into a deep sleep.

When he awoke the house was in semi-darkness. He got up feeling very stiff. He wondered if he had acquired a new set of joints where none had existed before. His spine felt like a board yet it wanted to bend in ways it never had.

Slowly, the little rodent moved out of the room, down the hall to the computer room and under the table to the hole-in-the-wall. He painfully hoisted himself over the baseboard and let himself fall into the food storage room behind the large jug and close to a sack where he could replenish his strength with some food.

When he was finally munching slowly on an apple he heard a voice from outside the sack.

"Is that you, Mousie?" whispered Rat. "I haven't seen you for most of the day. Where have you been?"

"Around," groaned the mouse. He meant to say "around and around" but couldn't bother with the details.

"The last I saw, you were after some jam. Did you get it?" asked Rat.

"I got in a jam alright," said the mouse rather softly.

"OK then, I'll see you in the morning. I've eaten my fill. Oh, did I mention I had a lovely afternoon chewing my way through another box? It was full of the softest material I have ever chewed! I was chewing faster than a paper shredder! I left quite a pile of tiny white flakes and I think I'll go back there tomorrow to have a nap on it. Did I mention I also had another encounter with the little yapper from upstairs? I had him going so badly. He was barking and in quite a tail spin when…"

"No," the mouse cut in. "You didn't mention and I don't care." Mouse had no energy to listen to another one of Rat's great stories.

Rat was insulted having been cut off in mid-story. Again Rat was thinking only about himself. He hadn't even bothered to look at the condition Mouse was in.

"Well, perhaps I'll tell you about it in the morning then. You don't seem very pleasant this evening!" And he sauntered off to find a spot to sleep in.

The little mouse groaned from his aches and fell to sleep in the sack, his belly only half-full.

14.
Near Death

The next morning, the little mouse rose to the reprimanding tones of Rat's voice: "I thought we had agreed we wouldn't sleep inside a food bag. It's too dangerous, you know, and..."

When Rat finally looked at the disheveled mouse, his mouth dropped.

"Why is your fur going one way and then another?" he asked. "Why is it either sitting flat or standing on end? You should spend more time taking care of yourself, my friend. Your body is your castle. Take a look at me!" Rat did a complete turn-around like a human model on the runway. "Can't you take more pride in how you look or do you expect me to do that for you too?"

Rat raised his paw towards the little mouse's back and was about to smooth out his mousey fur...

"Don't!" squealed the little frump. "No weight on me!"

"I don't understand. Do you mean not to 'wait' on you? You're right. I'm not your servant. You can clean *yourself* up but do it soon. I think I'll go and have a nap on the most luxuriously soft bed I've ever created. Oh, and do try to rid yourself of the smell of the laundry room. You smell as dreadful as a rose." And off went Rat through the hole-in-the-wall.

The little mouse was relieved to be left on his own. There wasn't a single spot on him that didn't ache from the tip of his nose to the end of his tail. Now, on top of that, his ears pulsed from the rat's lecturing.

He ate until he was full. Then he found a safe spot to sleep and he didn't come out that evening or the next. He slept on and on to give his body the time it needed to do some serious healing.

15.
Pestering the Poor Pooch

Meanwhile Rat had been busy. He hardly noticed that Mouse was nowhere to be found. Rat's life centered around whatever was best for Rat: either his survival or his entertainment. The woman and her dog gave Rat hours of challenge or fun.

He had a glorious time taunting the pup when he came downstairs to use his litter box. The mutt had done some growing in the last while but Rat was quite sure he would never get very big.

"He must be one of those lap-toys the humans seem to like so much. Frankly, I think he's a poor excuse for a dog. Yet I'm so pleased the woman has not brought a large and dangerous dog onto the place. This one is simply a plaything. I can get him in such a state he can't tell the difference between his front and his rear. When I tease him he'll jump at me, then he'll turn around at least ten times in a row before his eyes cross. By then, he's so dizzy he has to sit down before he falls down," Rat giggled to himself.

"Then I start all over again. I taunt him some more and he repeats the whole thing. By then the woman usually comes downstairs to pick him up and calm him. She can't figure out what has him in such a state. Oh, it's a great game for me," Rat chuckled. "I stay in hiding from the woman but the dog knows exactly where I am! By the time I'm done with him, he'll be half insane or so neurotic she'll wonder why she keeps him!" Rat gave an evil snicker. He was proud of his bad behavior.

The woman was not much bother. She only came into the storage room once or twice a week at most. She didn't need much food for herself and her wee dog. She didn't entertain much or if she did it didn't happen on the farm. She rarely left the pup at home by himself.

In the past the two rodents often heard her leaving the house. Then the truck could be heard as it moved down the road. Sometimes she was gone for an entire day, though she most often came home for night.

Twice a day she went outside to her farm animals and often stayed there for quite a while. Rat thought she might be giving flying lessons to her chickens. Maybe she rode the old horse. Or was she trying to train the goats to be more civil? He doubted that was possible. He didn't know what she did and he really didn't care.

Rat knew the routines in the house and that's what

kept him safe to do his exploring. 'Observant' was the word for that. Rat was very observant about things which affected his well-being and most often he only thought about his own well-being.

The woman thought the dog was responsible for any chewed items or scraps the two basement dwellers had left behind. She was very forgiving of anything her little gem might have done, which worked in Rat's favor.

Between eating his fill of a good variety of foods, vexing the dog, exploring the boxes and other fine items in the basement, and, of course, getting plenty of rest, Rat kept totally happy. His days were full of variety if he wanted it. Or he could do the 'same old' if that's what he chose.

He hadn't seen his mouse friend in several days now and that was okay too. Mouse had not been particularly pleasant to him the last time he had seen him. That was the way Rat saw it and Rat had a way of only seeing things through Rat's eyes. He had no idea what Mouse had been through.

16.
The Cords Strike Back

On a day when adventure was needed, Rat decided to hit the cords and hit them hard. He tumbled into their living room through the hole-in-the-wall. There he found a few cables and an interesting cord near the floor by the table. Sometimes he enjoyed the taste of plastic in his diet, and so he went at it. He was deep in thought about the wonderful life he had when he felt some slackness in the plastic as his teeth bore deeply into it.

His mind was so far away, he didn't realize he had chewed into the wire within the plastic. POOF! In an instant, he found himself being lifted off the ground by a great force! ZAP! He got such a jolt he could smell the sizzling of his own tail!

When his body came back down to the floor it bounced. He tumbled away from the wire which now sent sparks onto the floor. There was a click from the power box on the wall and all the usual sounds in the house stopped short. Whatever had just happened, Rat had gotten a charge he'd never experienced before. He heard the woman coming down the steps. In shock, he staggered behind a box which was filled with paper.

The woman pushed the lever on the power box but it clicked to the 'off' position again. Baffled by this, she examined the room to find the cause of the problem.

Luckily for poor Rat, she didn't have to look very hard. She saw the gnarled cord and unplugged it before trying the power box again. This time the switch stayed in place and Rat heard the humming sound from upstairs that had become so familiar, though he wasn't so sure the humming wasn't coming from inside his brain!

The woman stayed in the room to do a closer inspection of things. She picked up the chewed cord and nearly burst into tears with fear. She called to her pup. He bounded down the stairs, expecting she would pick him up and cuddle him. To his surprise, she shook her finger at him instead.

"You could have killed yourself by chewing that power cord! Oh, you are such a curious pup. How will I ever protect you from all the dangers?"

She sobbed and picked him up.

"What smells like burnt leather in here?" she sniffed. It must be from that power cord shorting out. I probably won't bother replacing it since I have my laptop." And with that, she carried the pup to the litter box and then headed back up the stairs.

17.
Porcupine?

Rat squeezed back into their kitchen through the hole. He saw the mouse inside a sack of wheat and went to join him. He had missed his little buddy, not having seen him in several days. Mouse glanced up, looked away, and then took another long look. He snickered and chuckled as only a mouse can do and then rolled on the floor with laughter. Every time he looked at Rat, he began laughing all over again. He laughed until he hurt.

"What's so funny?" inquired Rat, his ears still buzzing.

"Porcupine…" was all that the cackling mouse could get out.

"What are you talking about?" Rat asked. "Share the joke! What's all this about a porcupine?" Rat was now chuckling as well. He felt that he should join in on the laughter.

"Y-you," said the mouse between snickers. "F-fur! Standing up!" said the mouse, using his paw to clear the tears from his eyes. He had laughed so hard, he had cried. "And your t-tail!!"

Rat scrambled over to a tin can where he could catch his reflection. It was the closest thing he had to a mirror. He stopped chuckling. He looked at himself from the front. Then he went for a side view. Then he screwed his neck around to view himself from the back.

"You are right, Mousy! No matter which side I view myself from, I look perfectly round! My fur is standing on end. And my tail…Oh my poor tail! The end is hanging on by a thread!"

The tips of his ears were also burnt to a crisp. Rat knew the tips would eventually fall off and his ego was shattered. He had always taken such pride in his appearance. He would never be a perfect specimen again.

"What happened?" asked the mouse, who had finally regained his composure.

"I guess this is the effect of chewing through a power cord. It sent me straight up into the air," Rat explained. "And the smell of burnt leather! My poor tail and ears! Oh, I look dreadful. I suppose my fur will lie down after a while, but I didn't realize I had done so…"

Rat glanced back at the mouse only to find he was no longer listening. His hysterics long gone, his little friend was busily munching on the wheat.

As hungry as Rat was he couldn't eat a thing. He tried

licking. He tried preening. It was no use! He could not get his fur to lie flat and to shine as it had done in the past. Unhappily, and without supper, he slunk away and found a place to sleep. Feeling ashamed of his appearance, he didn't try to find his pal. He hadn't liked being laughed at. How was a rodent such as himself supposed to maintain a feeling of pride after this?

That night Rat dreamed of being sent straight into the air by a surge so strong it lit him on fire! No matter how many times he woke with a start, then drifted back to sleep, he would end up in the same bad dream. It was a dreadful night, one that he wouldn't forget too soon.

After a few weeks of healthy living, Rat started to look more like his old self again. His fur lay back down. His tail was shorter than it had been before but it was not unsightly. The ears, on the other hand, were now flat tops and a bit loppy. He looked like a new breed of rat, like the outcome of a scientist's prototype after years and years of crisscrossing genes. To keep his pride, Rat thought of himself as a one-of-a-kind new rat species. And that was that.

The little mouse had recovered surprisingly well from his washing machine ride, though he had not bothered to share his story with the rat. It would only have given Rat a reason to nag at him about climbing up the table leg in the first place. He had been goaded by the smell of jam, which happened to be his weakness. What was to be gained by telling Rat all about that? He knew enough about Rat by now to know that Rat only thought about himself. The mouse couldn't think of a single reason to share his bad experience, so he kept it to himself.

18.
Dancing with Danger

Upon Rat's next visit to the boxes he was startled by a dreaded shadow on the floor; a shape that he had seen before. He scrunched up his shaking body as if it was too late for any line of defense though something inside him was telling him to RUN! He quickly took cover behind a box! Nothing happened. Nothing chased him. He expected something to be clawing at the box. He waited. He cowered. Then his curiosity got the better of him as it usually did. He peered out and saw that the large shadow was still in the same place on the floor. It baffled him. He finally looked up at the basement window. Huddled against the outside of the window pane sat an old white cat. He had strayed from a nearby farm while on a hunt. The cat was warming himself with the draft which seeped through the leaky old basement window.

Now cats have an age-old history of war with rats and mice and it doesn't always show the rodents on the winning side. This was different though. This cat was on the other side of the glass. Rat gave a heavy sigh realizing he was totally safe.

"Now this could be fun," he thought.

He quickly darted out of the room, down the hall, into their living room and through the hole-in-the-wall. There he found Mouse gnawing away on the sack that held the apples.

"Follow me," puffed Rat. "You have to come see this. It gave me a fright at first but it's completely harmless."

Mouse stopped the chewing which he did simply to keep his teeth short and sharp.

"You sound breathless," he said looking up at Rat.

"Never mind that! Just follow me," said Rat, his breathing slowing down. "I promise it won't cause you any danger."

Mouse followed just to be a good sport. Most often he didn't care to be too close to Rat. He stayed a safe distance behind just in case Rat was feeling half-starved. [1]Once they were in the large storage room with all the boxes they stopped. Mouse still wasn't sure what all the fuss was about.

"Look up at that window," whispered Rat as he pointed. "Tell me what you see."

"Oh nasty! It's a cat!" exclaimed Mouse ready to dash for cover.

"I know!" Rat retorted with a grin. He put his paw

out to prevent Mouse from bolting. "But he can't hurt us. Watch this!"

Rat made faces. He danced around. He held his tail in his paw and circled it around like a lasso and sung, "You can't touch this!"

The scrawny Tom cat turned his head to watch. His ears perked up only slightly before he turned away, showing hardly any interest at all in the two clowns.

Once Mouse knew that the cat could not hurt them he joined in. The two rodents performed a brief dance on the floor. Mouse actually allowed himself to chortle and let loose. He followed Rat's lead in the dance.

Rat was into it now. He took Mouse by the paws and swung him around. Then with a swift move he swung him under his legs as if it was a rehearsed dance move. The two of them had a great moment together. They bumped their backsides and clapped with their paws. Now they swayed their hips and nudged up to each other and then spun outward while laughing and singing the whole time. They repeated this whole little routine several times. Then they ended off by doing the Hokey Pokey and they turned themselves around. After all, that's what it's all about! Rat loved the bit of bratty behavior he was seeing from Mouse. They were both show-offs at heart, he decided.

The next time they looked up to check on their audience the cat was gone. After a few laughs and rolls on the floor their fun was done. They headed back to the food storage room together with Rat laughing and retelling exactly what they had just done. They huffed from their exhaustion until their hearts regained their regular beats. They had a lovely meal of pumpkin seeds together feeling a new bond between them. One or the other kept bursting into short bouts of laughter. Neither of them had ever been so daring in the presence of a cat.

"We sure showed him that we weren't afraid," Rat said with a chuckle.

"Pretty much!" giggled Mouse.

"We make a pretty good team, wouldn't you say, little buddy?" asked Rat.

"Pretty much," replied the mouse.

After they finished their meal they went off to find a sleeping spot. They still broke into an occasional chuckle over the fun that they'd had together. Mouse slept beside Rat for the entire night. His dreams were more pleasant than they had been in the past. Not once did he imagine that a huge half-starved rat was stalking him.

19.
The Old Cat and Mouse Game

The old cat hadn't ventured very far that night. He may have slept in the chicken coop, in the bale stack or any other place that provided a bit of warmth. He had seen an easy meal in the basement of that house. He wasn't leaving until he had a chance to make a tasty breakfast out of the rodents.

The white stray had his chance that morning when the woman did her weekly litter box cleaning. She had taken the litter box out the hatch door and had left the interior door open so she wouldn't lock herself out. It was during those few innocent moments that the tom cat crept into the warmth of the basement and hid himself under an old covered rocker. The little mutt had stayed upstairs so there was no worry about a dog breaking his cover. The woman returned with a clean litter box, put it back in its usual spot, closed both doors and headed upstairs. The cat was in no hurry. He had time for a nice warm nap.

The cat was rousing himself with the first hint of a morning appetite when he saw the little mouse head into an open doorway. He took his time but kept one eye on the door opening. The mouse had not come back out so the cat, after several wakeful stretches, quietly crept to the door frame. He peered in to find a room of high benches and tools. He scanned the room with his sharp vision. He spied the little rodent on the floor chewing on an old cleaning rag. Silently the cat sat back in a crouched position. He took his time. He didn't make a move until he had scouted out the whole situation. If he could keep himself between the mouse and the door, he should have no trouble cornering the little varmint to go in for the deadly pounce.

He listened to the sounds of the little mouse's teeth gnawing away. He thought about his own teeth gnawing away on the mouse. This image made it impossible for him to hold out any longer! He flexed his claws as if to sharpen them. He curled his spine to ensure that his own body wouldn't let him down once the fun began. After two quick steps he POUNCED! He had the little thing under his paw but the hold wasn't very good. He had captured him just above the tail. The cat wasn't the least bit worried about the near miss though. This was part of the fun for him.

Now the meal planning would begin in earnest. He was about to bring his other paw around to secure his hold when the mouse squeezed out of the weak hold and darted rapidly toward the corner of the room, leaving a spot of blood behind him.

"A corner is an even better location," thought the old tom cat. He showed his vicious teeth in what looked like a wicked smile.

Mouse was terrified! He had become too relaxed in the basement. He hadn't been cautious. He was quite sure this was the same cat they had made fun of the night before. He had no time to delve into any regret for his naughty behaviour.

The cat had taken another step toward him.

"Can't touch this, eh?" the cat snarled. "Let's see you dance now!"

Mouse couldn't see how he could get out of this one. His eyes darted quickly from one corner of the room to the other, hoping to find a solution to his problem. He had backed himself into a corner without the faintest idea as to what his next move would be.

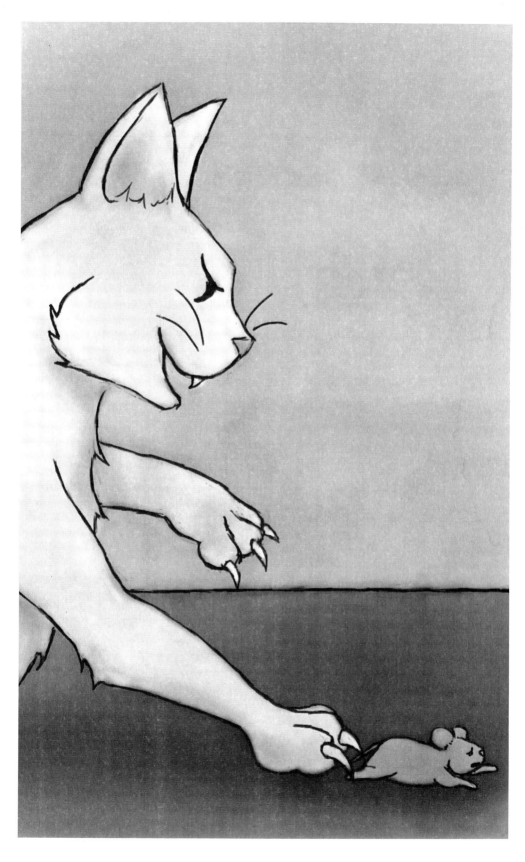

20.
Rat to the Rescue

Meanwhile, Rat had finished his breakfast of dried corn and had cleaned himself up for another day in his heaven. He decided he would find out what Mouse was up to this morning. He made his way out the hole in the wall. He thought he heard a thud against the wall in the next room.

"That must be Mouse. I wonder what he's doing. Perhaps he would like to try some more dancing this morning." He snickered at the memory of the night before.

He slithered under the door and tried a few new dance moves as he made his way down the hall to the tool room. He caught an unpleasant odour for a second but didn't think much of it. He turned at the door entrance and abruptly he halted! He had to blink twice before he believed his eyes! It was the cat about to strike. He looked again. There was the mouse huddled in a corner. There was blood! He had to help!

Now it is a fact that cats like to play with their kill.

They prefer to carry it around for a while. They like to set it down while the victim still has some life left. The cat really enjoys its prey's final attempt to escape. It's a way to extend the hunt.

The cat crouched for his final pounce. Rat thought quickly. The cat flew and Rat burst into action. The cat was in mid-air when Rat distracted him, his tail going round in the lasso motion, a copied move from the night before. "Want a piece of me?" he called.

Cat was slightly side-tracked as he glanced over at the rat. When he came down he missed his bull's eye aim by a fraction but he had pinned the mouse once more. The squeals and screeches that came from Mouse made it obvious he was injured. Now the cat was feeling greedy. The mouse was disabled enough that he couldn't move. Cat thought he might go after the larger prey and still end up with both.

Rat was already in motion. He sped down the hallway. Even so, the cat was right behind him and making great gains. Rat was flat out when he slid under the computer room door. The mangy cat was airborne with claws outstretched when he hit the door straight on. He fell to the floor with a SCREECH and a BANG! Rat got up on all fours within the safety of his living room.

The sounds had alerted the woman upstairs and Rat could hear her running down the stairs. He panted as he peeked under the door to see her feet approach.

She screamed at seeing the strange cat whose nose was slightly flattened from hitting the door so solidly.

The woman mumbled and swore as she ran to open the doors to the hatch. She tried to coax the alien cat toward the concrete steps and outside but the cat was uncooperative. Perhaps he was too dizzy to move. Perhaps he wouldn't leave without retrieving his breakfast from the tool room. Perhaps he was in shock! It wasn't until she swept at him with the long handled weapon that he moved at all.

Rat could hear that the dog had joined into the great ado. The two of them, master and mutt, ran around cutting the cat off as he tried to re-enter the tool room. They shooed him this way and that until he finally raced up the hatch steps and back outside.

Rat heard the woman close both doors and head back to her upstairs domain. She was carrying her little canine and doing a bit of heavy breathing herself. All was quiet.

Rat made his way through the hole in the wall. He sat and panted for a moment before the thought of food even came to him. He ate just a little to settle himself and then found a napping spot behind some jars up on the second shelf. As usual, he was thinking only of himself.

When he woke he looked down to the floor to see the mouse drinking from the leaky jug.

"You look a little worse for wear," said Rat, as he made his way down from the shelf.

Mouse made no comment as he licked at the blood on his backside. Once Rat was down he examined the little one's injuries. After a thorough inspection he said, "It's not too bad. You'll survive."

"Thanks. You saved me." That was all the mouse said.

"Don't mention it," gloated Rat, as he tended to his own fur. "You're a good dance partner and I couldn't imagine never doing our dance again."

They ate supper together. The near death incident was not mentioned – not ever again.

The little mouse healed much quicker from his latest injury than he had from his ride in the wash machine.

21.
A Sad Farewell

The animals knew that spring was coming. They could feel it in their bones. Besides that, there were all the regular signs. There were an increasing number of sunlight hours. The heavy frost that had lined the windows all winter long had now melted. By looking up and out the window the rodents saw the return of some of the birds on the highest tree branches, which would soon be in full bud. Spring was a wonderful time of year, especially since it led up to summer, which was by far the best time of year.

The two of them had not suffered from any lack of food sources. Well, they might have gotten a little bored of eating the same types all winter, but it was a great step up from not knowing where their next meal might come from. Perhaps they'd become a bit spoiled.

One day, the woman spent longer than usual in the basement. Rat wanted to go and see what she was doing, but his instincts told him not to push his luck. He couldn't resist peeking around a corner though. He discovered she had opened not only the door to the mutt's litter box but also the trap door that led outside. Rat recalled that it was the one through which he had entered the house early last winter. She carried the litter box up the steps and out the hatch door and she didn't bring it back in. She took her long handled weapon and began to sweep out the hatch space.

When she had finished, she left her weapon leaning against the wall and proceeded to remove some of the old boxes of junk from the storage room. These were taken up the hatch steps and out the door as well. She was gone for quite a while. If either rodent had the desire to leave the comforts of the basement and head for the great outdoors, this would have been the perfect chance.

The pup had gone out the front door of the house from the upstairs. Every once in a while Rat saw him pressing his nose against a basement window. He was practicing his endless barking while running from window to window.

"You can't see me," whispered Rat. "You might know I'm here but you're not smart enough to spot me through a dirty window, especially when I haven't moved a muscle."

The little dog followed the woman into the basement. Rat retreated to another room but he could hear the woman going on.

"You won't need a litter box any longer, my baby," she explained. "From now on you'll do your business out-of-doors. Now come along upstairs and I'll give you a milk bone. You can chew it on the front steps in the warm sunshine." She picked him up and the two of them hurried up the stairs and the door closed at the top.

"Blah blah blah blah," mocked Rat. "Does she actually think he understands a single thing she says? If she wants to have a meaningful conversation perhaps she should give me a try. I understand the languages of many, many animals and quite a bit of people tongue. Oh well, thank goodness they're gone and thank goodness for the end of that litter box! I'll have to work very hard to cover up that lingering odor with my own smells!"

Rat was jarred from his thoughts by the sound of crashing glass that came from their basement kitchen. He scurried off down the hall to find out its cause. When he entered, he found the mouse up on a high shelf looking down at a jar of jam he had pushed off onto the floor. He was now making a hasty descent as he licked his lips.

"Jam! I can smell it!" exclaimed the mouse, racing for the sticky pool.

"Yah, well, the last time you went after some jam I didn't see you for days and it changed you in ways I can't describe," said Rat. "Besides, you're only going to get us…"

The upstairs door had opened and he could hear

the woman running down the stairs. Rat ran from the food storage room and watched through the hole-in-the-wall. The mouse, on the other hand, couldn't tear himself away from the jam. Either that or he was glued to the floor in the sticky goo.

It wasn't until the woman opened the storage room door and spotted the little jam addict that the mouse high-tailed it. And not a second too soon! With her long handled weapon in hand, she chased the poor frightened mouse out the door; then down the hall and up the steps leading to the upstairs. Every few seconds the weapon came down with a bang and Rat could only imagine the worst!

The chasing and banging went on for the better part of the evening. Furniture moved and slid across the floor. Dishes rattled from the great chase. The woman's footsteps could be heard from one end of the house to the other. Pictures fell from the walls following the weapon's thrust. Ornaments crashed and broke upon hitting the floor. The pup squealed in all the excitement. Finally, the outside door slammed shut with a final BANG! Then there was silence.

That's the end of my poor little cousin," sighed Rat. "And I was just starting to enjoy the little gaffer. Perhaps I should say a few words in his memory. Let me think…Mouse loved jam. It was his downfall and the cause of his death. He was a good dance partner. There! Done with that."

22.
Spring Cleaning

No sooner had he finished his short memorial than he heard the woman coming down the steps again. She returned to the storage room with a bucket of water and a mop. She got busy cleaning up the jam and disposing of the broken glass.

"I thought I saw a mouse turd down here," she said.

"Mouse turd sounds like mass turd sounds like mustard," snickered Rat softly. All of the excitement had put him in a giddy state.

"Tomorrow I'll do a complete spring cleaning down here. And to think I've been blaming that wretched smell on Bimbo and his litter box. It wasn't him at all."

Rat nearly split his seams! He muffled his laughter by covering his mouth with his paw just in case he couldn't contain it.

"Bimbo! She has named him Bimbo. That is too perfect for words. The dog is an absolute BIMBO!" Rat chuckled.

"I wonder if there is more than one mouse down here. I guess I'll find out tomorrow," sighed the woman. "That's enough for tonight."

She stomped back up the stairs with her cleaning weapons in hand.

"What a pity," said Rat. "I would have enjoyed a bit of that jam myself if she'd left it. I'm not an addict but a nibble would have been nice. Oh well."

Rat stood up on two feet and did a little jig as he made up a new song.

"Bimbo, Bumbo you call yourself a dog?

Mimbo, Mumbo you're dumber than a log.

Bimbo, Bambo if I had to have your name

I'd feel so ashamed because it's just… so… lame!"

Oh, where was Mouse when he needed him? They really could have had fun with this one, thought Rat. He thought back to the silly dance they had invented together.

Rat had no one to keep him warm for even part of the night. He could have become sad over the situation but that wasn't his nature. Besides, he had concerns far bigger. The woman would be back the next day with her weapons of mass destruction. If he wasn't careful they could be 'weapons of Rat's destruction'!

He knew that a plan would come to him. He was

after all a genius. He would sleep on it and the plan would be there for him by morning. That's the way it had always worked.

*W*hen morning came he had an early breakfast. It would be a shame to have to part with this perfect living arrangement but life goes on and things do change. That was all his brain had come up with while he slept; this was the only revelation he'd woken with. 'Life goes on and things change'. If his life went on, he should be happy enough!

He had finished his breakfast and was having a good long drink from the leaky jug when he heard the woman preparing her ammunition. She came down the stairs, bringing the little yelper with her.

"Bimbo, Bombo, Bumbo…Mimbo, Mombo, Mumbo…" thought Rat to himself. "I wonder why she didn't just call him Yelper. He could be Mommy's little Yelper, something like Santa's little helper…"

Rat ended his nonsense and quickly dove through the hole-in-the-wall as he heard the woman enter the storage room.

The woman just stood for a while. She looked here and there and moved a few things around. Rat couldn't see all that was going on because the jug was blocking his view. He could hear though.

The woman had started some serious cleaning. She removed all the jars from a high shelf and wiped it down. Rat could hear little turd pellets dropping to the floor as she slid the cloth over the shelf. She stopped and went out of the room and back up the stairs. He could hear her cursing about the turds and mess that she had to clean.

"Is she done? Was that it? Is that all there is to spring cleaning? Perhaps I could do some myself if it's that easy," whispered Rat.

After a few minutes the woman returned, and this time she had a machine with her which she plugged into a socket. The machine roared loudly as it sucked up all the turds.

The woman was on a roll now. She emptied a few shelves and used the machine to suck them clean. She wiped the shelves with the wet cloth. She wiped the jars and put them back on the shelves. This went on and on and Rat got bored of watching.

"No, I've changed my mind," he decided. "I don't think I'll do any spring cleaning. It's no fun at all and it takes up too much time. Besides, it's being done for me."

23.
Farewell Rat

Rat made his way into the storage room thinking he might start on a new box. Suddenly the little yelper was right behind him. Rat quickly took cover under the old covered rocking chair. The dog began his pitiful barking, running around the sides of the chair until his voice was shrieking.

"Wuzzup, dog?" Rat teased.

The dog was in a rage now, which made Rat's grin even bigger.

The woman came to see what all the fuss was about. She picked up her little Bimbo and calmed him with her cooing tone. Then she went back upstairs and Bimbo went with her. Rat could hear her open the front door to let the dog outside.

"Oh, too bad," thought Rat. "I could've gone a few rounds with him this morning. We haven't had a good bout in a while now."

When she came back down she stood silently at the

entrance to the room with all the old furniture and boxes. She sniffed a few times. She moved a few boxes, and then opened one that Rat had particularly enjoyed. That was when she lost it!

"Oh, no! My grandmother's wedding dress has been destroyed!" she cried. "It's been pulverized. It's been chewed to bits!"

She threw the entire box to the side and opened some others, spewing out words that were far too nasty to repeat and some that Rat had never even heard before. She opened the hatch, went up the steps and opened the trap door as well. She carried box after box outside, mumbling and ranting about what had happened to her special things. Her little mutt joined her outside for a moment, his tail moving rapidly from side to side with excitement.

All this time, Rat had not moved. He saw that the only boxes she wasn't carrying out were the ones he hadn't explored yet.

"I'm glad she's getting rid of the ones I'm done with," Rat said quietly. "I'll know right where to start the next time."

After a long while of opening, examining and carrying out boxes, she finished the job. She restacked the few boxes she was keeping, then she sighed with exhaustion. She sat in the old rocker and had a rest. Rat had a rest right beneath her. Bimbo must have stayed outside, as he was nowhere to be seen or heard.

After her rest, the woman went back into the storage room and started the sucking machine again. The idea that someone could carry on all day with such a boring task made Rat quite curious. Surely something more interesting had to happen. He hurried back to the room with the cords where he could watch from the hole-in-the-wall.

His head was right through the hole when the woman turned off the machine. She bent down on her knees and slid the jug out of the way. Before Rat knew what had happened, the two of them were face to face! "EEK, Yuck, oohh!" The woman had let out such a scream, Rat piddled right there on the spot!

He turned to run but there behind him was the dog, which gave him such a fright Rat became airborne and leapt right over the pup! Rat ran and the dog chased him with hysterical screechy barks.

Rat ducked under the old rocking chair. The dog's paws reached for him! He rushed for cover beneath a low table but the little Bimbo was right behind him again!

Rat was running out of hiding spots! He quickly dashed beneath that same old couch which had given him protection the first time he'd entered the house. He crouched and took a few deep gasps to regain his breath. He tried to decide his next move while the dog growled and pawed as if he would come right through the old couch! Rat had never heard the dog so fierce before!

Now Rat could hear the voice of the woman who had followed them into the room: "Get him, Bimbo! End the life of that smelly rodent! I'll go get my broom!" She ran off while her dog kept up his same pattern of growl, nip, bark and scratch, growl, nip, bark and scratch. Bimbo was heated up and prepared to KILL!

Rat saw that the hatch and trap door above were open and he made a quick decision. With all his gusto, he raced through the doorway, up the concrete steps and into the freedom of the great outdoors. The dog was nipping at his tail as he ran across the yard! He ran past the henhouse where the chickens flew into an uproar!

He ran and ran until he was safe inside of the goat pen. The pup stayed on the other side of the fence, where he sat panting from his great chase.

"I thought I told you never to come back here, you rat!" said the old mother goat. The Nanny took the opportunity to stay true to her promise. She picked Rat up by his blunt ended tail and whisked him high over the fence. She waited to hear the sound of a crack. Rat spun as he flew through the air. He rather enjoyed this new flying experience. He landed on a soft pile of material with hardly a sound. After a moment, he gave himself a shake. To his surprise he felt fine. Thank goodness for soft landings.

Looking around him, he saw it was the same white material he had enjoyed chewing in the basement. He looked again, and to his joy all of the things the woman had removed from the basement were sitting in a big heap under and around him. It was like moving the winter home outdoors, which made it a summer home!

As he raised his head to get a better view of the junk heap he saw the little dog returning to the farm house. His tail was wagging proudly. He bounded toward the woman who stood just outside the house, leaning on her broom handle.

"Good for you Bimbo! That's two out of two! You are my little hero!" she said.

Rat watched as they both went back down the steps and into the basement.

"Is she crazy?" thought Rat. "Who is the real hero here? Does she know what I've just been through? I'm the hero! I'm the survivor! I'm the smart one!"

24.
Hello Again

Rat wasn't at all bruised from his sailing experience and soft landing. He was able to move about just as soon as he cleaned himself off. He took a very short rest to catch his breath. Then he darted around in the pile. He dove in and buried himself in garbage and in pure joy!

All around him were the things he loved. It was fantastic! To his surprise, the woman had even thrown out the sacks of wheat, oatmeal, dried corn and apples because they were old and all had bits of rodent turds in them. He made his way toward the sacks. All the excitement had given him an appetite. He climbed toward the bag of oatmeal, and there he heard a familiar sound. After a quick search he spotted his pal whose cheeks were bulging.

"Hello Mousie! I'm so glad to see you! I thought something dreadful had happened to you. Tell me, how did you ever get out of that house alive?"

Mouse didn't bother to finish the food in his mouth.

He simply said, "The same way I got in - through the door."

"Right. Well, you couldn't have given a shorter explanation! You are a mouse more mighty than I ever would have imagined! Like me, you have a strong desire to survive." Rat exclaimed. "I'm half-starved. Can you move over a bit so that we can share the wealth?"

"Yikes! Not this again!" thought Mouse. He let Rat into the bag and made sure he remained near the opening.

"If I do say so myself, and I do, I am one smart rat! I outsmarted the human, her dog, a mangy old cat – and I did that for your sake as you may recall." He stopped long enough to munch on the oatmeal. "I even ended up better off because of a goat that thought she would end my life with one flip! That flip put me right here where I want to be: in a new summer home with you," said Rat with some emotion. Then he continued: "You know, maybe there's a thing or two I could learn from you, little friend."

"Like what?" asked Mouse.

"Well, although you didn't save my life or anything as GREAT as that, I enjoy you. You are a friend," Rat confessed, as he took another little nibble.

"Are we really friends?" questioned Mouse.

"Golly yes! And don't you forget it!" Rat said with

the deepest emotion he could come up with.

"But you have always threatened that if you were half-starved you'd eat me!" explained Mouse. "I have never felt very comfortable around you."

"Oh that? That's just an old saying that I kind of like. I wouldn't eat my best friend. If I did, then who would I dance with?" snickered Rat.

The little mouse's jaw slowly turned upward in the shape of a wee smile. He felt some relief from the words Rat had just spoken. Perhaps Rat was a friend even though he was a very talkative and selfish friend.

Rat cleared his throat, preparing for what might be a very long story. "Let me tell you how I got out. By the way, are we not the most fortunate pair to find our mother lode in the great outdoors? Our winter home just became our summer home! ... Now, what was I saying? ... Oh yes, I was about to tell you of my great escape. I was ..."

Mouse sensed he would be hearing the long, detailed and heroic story of Rat's escape many times in the days to come. Feeling quite ready for a nap, he made a quiet exit from the bag without Rat taking the slightest notice. Rat probably carried on with his story for the better part of the day and well into the night.

THE END

(Endnotes)

1 Final Notes

Many thanks go to Gordon Pengilly for editing and suggesting that extra chapter.

Thanks also to Connie for her encouragement and many kind words.

Thanks to Doug for willingly reading the novel again and again as it came about.

Thanks to Nick for helping me through all the computer struggles regarding the illustrations.

Finally a big thanks goes to Marcy Trockstad for her wonderful illustrations which brought the novel to life. If you want to hire her she can be reached at: marcytrockstad@gmail.com

If you have any questions or you just want to chat about the book you can find me on Facebook or at eupengilly7@live.ca.

Rat was not intended to be a totally likeable character. The hero of this story has many traits of a villain. That's what makes him questionable or 'food for thought'. It also makes him more believable because most of us have traits of both.

A comprehensive teaching package is available from eupengilly7@live.ca.

If you are curious about Mouse and his withdrawn nature look for the picture book:

WHY THE LITTLE MOUSE DOESN'T TALK (VERY MUCH) – A Modern Fable - coming out next year.

THERE'S A RAT IN THIS CITY is in the works. The story begins where RAT left off. The woman removes the junk heap from her yard and with it goes Rat and Mouse. They run up against gangsta' rats at the city dump. They encounter huge, lazy rats living under a fast food restaurant. Mouse's jam addiction causes further difficulties while Rat tries to outsmart the city dwellers. Wait for it.

Printed in Canada